MATE & RIX
ESCAPE BOREDOM

by Jolie Curran

illustrated by
Frans Vischer

~~~~~~~~~~

For Lariah, Larissa, and Stuart,
who remind me it takes courage to turn dreams into reality; and

For Marsh and Lucille,
who would have told everyone 'Don't wait. Do it now.'
~JSC

To my wife, Jennifer, high school English teacher, and teachers everywhere.
~FV

The author would also like to thank Jennifer Rees
for being a supportive and honest editor.

Copyright © 2022 by Jolie S. Curran

First hardcover edition May 2023
For bulk purchases, please contact jolie@mateandrix.com.

Illustrated by Frans Vischer
Edited by Jennifer Rees
Title and copyright page layout by Patricia Joseph

ISBN: 979-8-9858672-0-6 (paperback)
ISBN: 979-8-9858672-1-3 (kindle)
ISBN: 979-8-9858672-2-0 (EPUB)
ISBN: 979-8-9858672-3-7 (hardcover)

www.mateandrix.com

There were no cats to tease. No dogs to please.

"Yes, a cozy fort."
"Inside we can play games."

"And tell stories."

"Let's find a good place for a fort!"

But somebody already lived there.

"This one looks fun.
And nobody lives here."

"It's all glass, Mate. That's not cozy."

"This could be cozy."

"And no one lives here."

"Pennies!"

"We could use the pennies to
fill the holes, Mate."

"Ten, twenty, thirty, forty, fifty.
That's a lot of holes."

So Mate and Rix went to work.

"Rollin' rollin' rollin',
        get the pennies rollin'."

"Lining up twenty-nine."

"Lining up eighteen more."

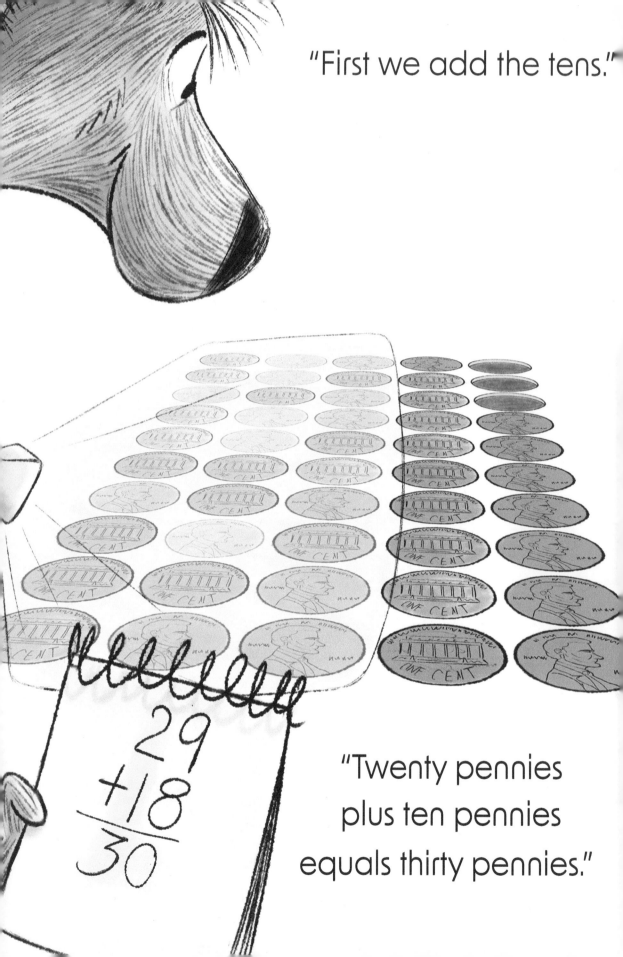

"First we add the tens."

"Twenty pennies
plus ten pennies
equals thirty pennies."

"Next step, Rix, is to add the ones."

"Nine pennies plus eight pennies is seventeen pennies."

"Let's add it together!"

"Three more to make fifty."

Mate and Rix scurried about. In and out, round about, up and down, here, there, and everywhere, until...

There was only one thing left to do.

About Partial-Sums Addition Algorithm

There are various methods people use for multi-digit addition. One of these is called the partial-sums method, which is the method Mate and Rix use in this book.

You may have a favorite method of your own. Even if you do, learning and teaching partial-sums addition method helps the student to develop number sense, algebraic reasonioning, and mental math strategies.

Students learn to:
. Identify the place value of digits in the numbers
. Write numbers in expanded notation
. Visualize the construction of multi-digit numbers

For parents, this is an excellent method to help their child build math confidence. This method can be used to understand their homework and revise errors.

How Partial-Sums Addition works

The partial-sums addition algorithm works by calculating one place value column at a time. Then, adding up those partial-sums to calculate the total. This is a flexible method Students may perform this method left-to-right or right-to-left and compute the correct tot

Example

Solve 638 + 946

Step 1: Think about the expanded notation of the numbers being added.

638 = 600 + 30 + 8

946 = 900 + 40 + 6

Step 2: Add the hundreds column.

	638
	+ 946
600 + 900	1500

Step 3: Add the tens column.

	638
	+ 946
600 + 900	1500
30 + 40	70

Step 4: Add the ones column.

	638
	+ 946
600 + 900	1500
30 + 40	70
8 + 6	+ 14

Step 5: Add the partial-sums to compute the total.

	638
	+ 946
600 + 900	1500
30 + 40	70
8 + 6	+ 14
Total	1584

638 + 946 = 1,584

The partial-sums addition method breaks down large numbers into more manageable pieces. This develops a strong conceptual understanding of place value and multi-digit computation.

Visit mateandrix.com for FREE guides, giveaways, and information about new book releases.